W9-AVS-921

JASPER'S DAY

For Jay — M.B.P.

To the Kniftons, both the two-legged and the four-legged, with love.

Many thanks to River and his family, Dave Cobb and Kayleigh — J.W.

Kids Can Press acknowledges the financial support of the Ontario Arts Council, the Canada Council for the Arts and the Government of Canada, through the BPIDP, for our publishing activity.

Published in Canada by
Kids Can Press Ltd.
29 Birch Avenue
Toronto, ON M4V 1E2

Published in the U.S. by
Kids Can Press Ltd.
2250 Military Road
Tonawanda, NY 14150

www.kidscanpress.com

The artwork in this book was rendered in chalk pastels on colored paper.
The text is set in Esprit Book.

Edited by Debbie Rogosin
Designed by Julia Naimska
Printed and bound in Hong Kong, China, by Book Art Inc., Toronto

This book is smyth sewn casebound.

CM 02 0 9 8 7 6 5 4 3 2 1

National Library of Canada Cataloguing in Publication Data

Parker, Marjorie Blain, 1960–

Jasper's day

ISBN 1-55074-957-9

1. Dogs — Juvenile fiction. 2. Death — Juvenile fiction.
I. Wilson, Janet, 1952– II. Title.

PS8581.A7612J38 2002 jC813'.54 C2001-903686-8
PZ7.P22272Ja 2002

Kids Can Press is a

Entertainment company

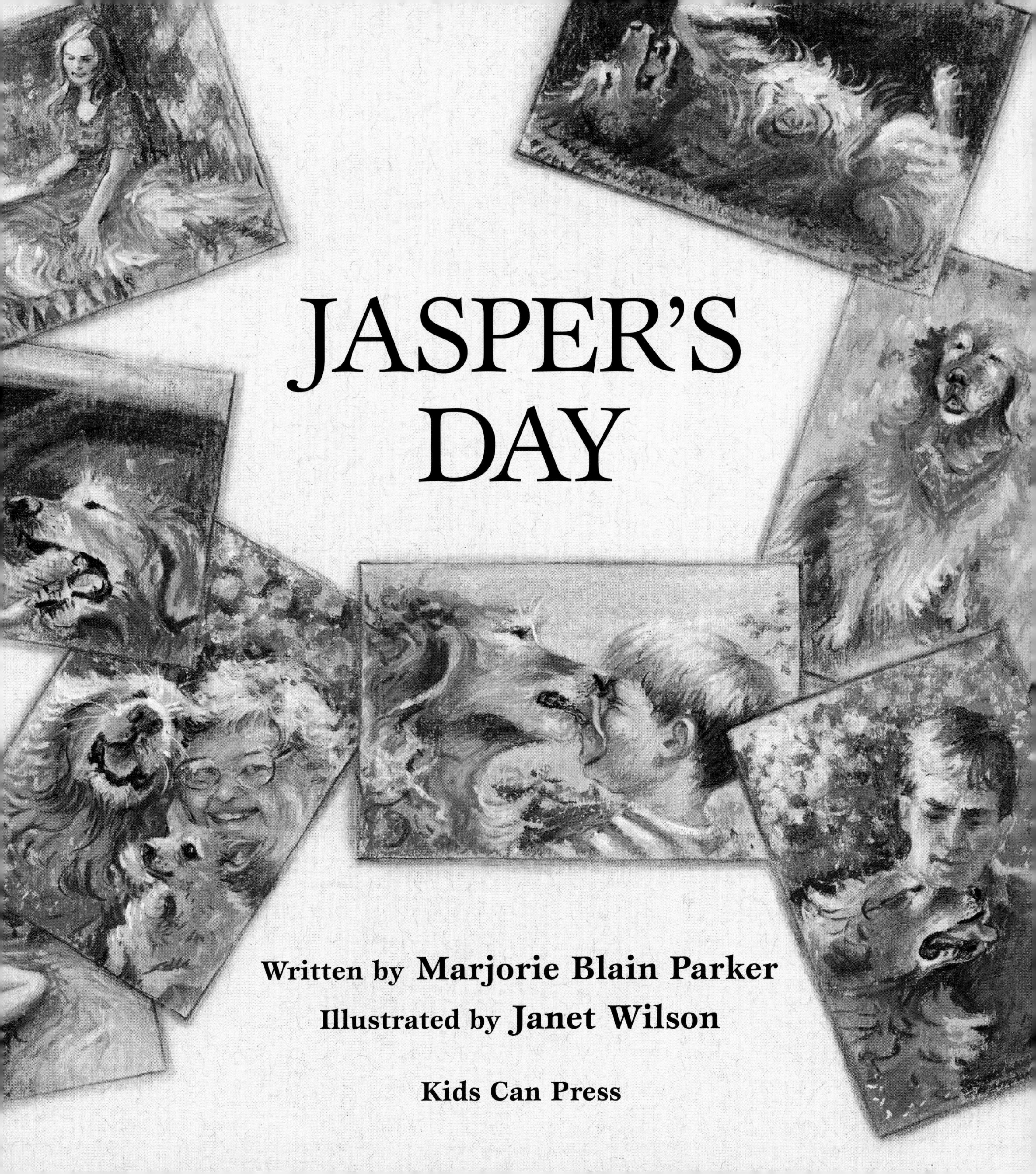

JASPER'S DAY

Written by **Marjorie Blain Parker**
Illustrated by **Janet Wilson**

Kids Can Press

Jasper is still sleeping when I wake up. He sleeps a lot these days. He's sprawled out, taking up half the bed like he always does. I nudge him gently with my foot, but he keeps dozing. That's okay. He can sleep in. Today is his day.

Today we are celebrating Jasper's Day. It was my idea. Mom and Dad are staying home from work. I'm staying home from school. Everything we do will be in honor of Jasper — sort of like a birthday. But it isn't Jasper's birthday, and I tell myself not to think about what day it really is.

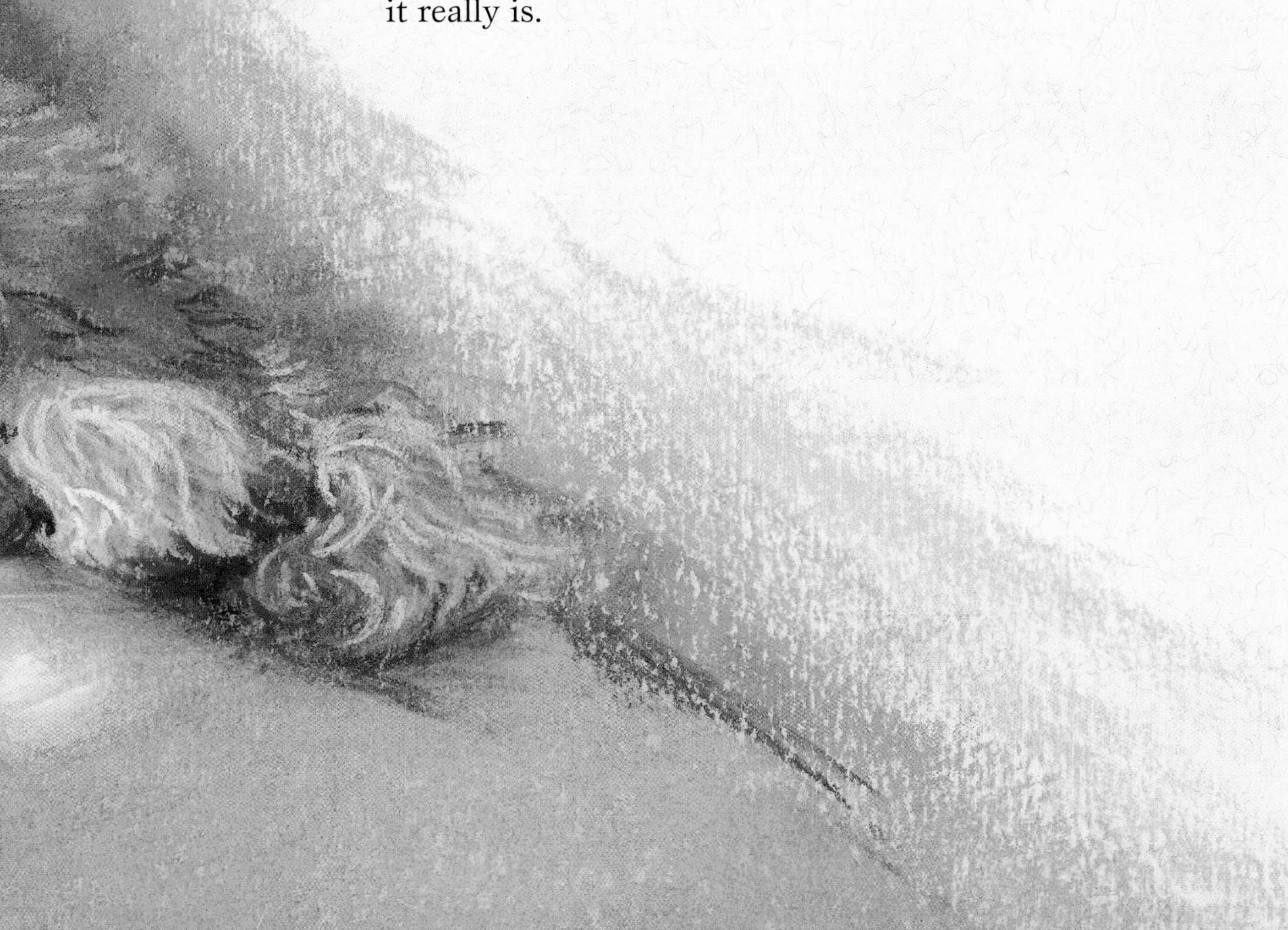

I hear Mom and Dad in the kitchen. I get dressed quickly and run down to see them. But halfway there I remember, and I go back to make sure the big beanbag chair is in the right spot. Jasper needs a soft place to land when he gets out of bed.

Mom and Dad are making breakfast. Both of them smile when they see me in the doorway.

“Morning, Riley,” Mom says. She tries to sound cheerful.

We hug.

Jasper’s cancer has gotten really bad. Mom and Dad say there’s only one thing to do. I know they’re right. We can’t let him suffer. But I’m not ready. This will be the hardest day of my life.

Pretty soon there's a big THUD from my room. We all grin. Jasper's up.

Breakfast is very merry. Jasper must wonder what's gotten into us. He's used to mooching for scraps, but this morning he gets his own serving of favorites — scrambled eggs with cheese, and bacon. The eggs are soft, so there's no need for chewing. Mom tucks a couple of pain pills into them, and he swallows his medicine without even knowing it. The bacon goes down in two big gulps. We haven't seen Jasper eat like this in months.

"I guess dog food doesn't compare to people food," I say. Mom and Dad chuckle. I'm glad they're laughing. I didn't think we'd be able to laugh today. I didn't think we'd want to eat either. But Jasper's appetite is contagious. I have a second helping!

After we've cleared the table and washed the dishes, we load up the van. I ask Mom if I can bring the camera.

"Good thinking," she says.

Dad sets Jasper on the back seat with me. His hind legs are so stiff with arthritis that he can't get in by himself anymore. He's happy to be going for a ride, though. Always is. He even sticks his head out the window to feel the wind on his face. Just like the old days.

"Don't you dare fart," I warn him sternly. Old dogs can be pretty smelly, and Jasper is no exception.

We're going to the stream. When he was younger, Jasper loved to swim and fetch sticks there. It's been a year or two since we've gone, and I wonder if he'll remember it. The drive only takes half an hour — but Jasper's snoozing on my lap by the time we pull off the road. The gravel crunching under the tires wakes him. His tail starts wagging. He knows exactly where we are.

Mom spreads out the arrowhead blanket under a big old fir, while Dad and I coax Jasper down to the stream. Dad tosses a stick into the water. Jasper takes a drink, but no way is he getting in! He barks at us. “WOOF!”

“I don’t blame you, boy. It’s pretty chilly.” Dad smiles. “You couldn’t keep Jasper dry in the old days,” he says. “And he’d chase a stick if you threw it off the top of a mountain.”

I remember those days. They weren’t that long ago.

Jasper shuffles back to Mom and the cool shade. Dad and I comb the bank of the stream looking for skippers. I'm pretty good with the right kind of stone. Dad is awesome.

But soon we head back to the tree. I stretch out on the blanket, next to Jasper. Two lazybones. In the branches above, a chipmunk chatters, scolding us for invading his forest. Jasper doesn't notice. His eyes and ears don't work so well anymore. I breathe in the tingly scent of fresh pine growth. What about Jasper's nose? I've never thought about that before. Has getting old dulled his sense of smell, too?

I scratch his grizzled chin, memorizing every little detail about him. "Hey, Mom — photo opportunity," I say. I want a picture of us like this.

We rest a while longer, and then it's time to go. Jasper's Day is flying by.

Our next destination is Grandma's house, but on the way we stop at The Big Scoop for a treat. We've been bringing Jasper here for years. Dad orders the usual for Jasper and himself — butterscotch ripple. He says it's Jasper's favorite, but I know whose favorite it really is.

Dad talks to the owner for a minute, and the next thing you know he's coming outside with us to see Jasper. There are still people in the store waiting to buy ice cream! "I'll just be a minute, folks," he tells them. "I have important business outside with one of my loyal customers." Boy, am I glad I brought the camera.

Grandma comes out to greet us when we pull up. She's been waiting.

Her dog, Nikki, barks with joy when she sees Jasper. Her best pooch pal! She runs up and licks him on the mouth. Dog kisses — yuck!

Jasper is tired, and Dad carries him most of the way to the sun porch. "We can't stay long, Mom," he says.

Grandma rubs Jasper on the chest. Jasper loves her massages. He manages to roll over enough to get one paw in the air. His silky tail thumps on the rug. I wish we could stay like this forever.

But soon, too soon, Mom checks her watch. “It’s time to get to the clinic,” she whispers to Dad.

He nods. “Just a few more minutes,” he says.

How about fifty thousand more, I think. I'm still not ready. This day has been too short. I hide my face in Jasper's fur and fight back tears. I don't want to say good-bye.

But suddenly, Jasper whimpers. The pills must be wearing off. He's hurting. It's time to go after all.

A surprising thought hits me. Maybe Jasper's ready.

I feel Dad's hand on my shoulder, warm and strong. "Riley," he says. I take a deep breath and then get to my feet. Together, we lift Jasper.

Dad drops Mom and me off at home. I hold Jasper for the last time. "Good-bye, buddy," I whisper in his ear. "You're the best dog in the whole world." He licks my cheek. He knows it.

And then they are gone.

The veterinarian is going to give Jasper a shot. It will be quick and gentle. For Jasper, it will be just like going to sleep. He won't be asleep, though. Jasper will be dead. I stand there crying. Mom, too.

Dad brings Jasper home wrapped in the arrowhead blanket. We go out to the backyard, over by the blue spruce. Dad dug a hole there yesterday. He lays Jasper in the ground.

We put some things in with him — an old chew toy, a stick, his water dish, a picture of our family. We stand there and talk about Jasper from start to finish. We cry some, but we laugh plenty, too. Then Dad shovels the dirt back into the grave, until Jasper is buried in the earth. We stay there until the shadows start getting long.

The house seems hollow without Jasper in it. My bed feels empty without him. My chest aches. Mom and Dad got Jasper before I was even born. He's always been in my life. Tomorrow will be my first day ever without him. I'm going to miss Jasper so, so much.

I look at our picture on my nightstand. I think about all the ones we took today, and it gives me an idea. I'll make a memory book of Jasper's life. I can work on it over the summer.

I close my eyes. I was right. Today *was* the hardest day of my life.

But I'm glad we celebrated Jasper's Day. Because it was a good day, too.